Le Lion et la Souris
Une Fable d'Aesop

D1066723

The Lion and the Mouse
an Aesop's Fable

Jan Ormerod

French translation by Annie Arnold

Très loin, il y a très longtemps, alors qu'un lion était allongé endormi, une petite souris courut le long de sa queue. Elle courut sur son dos et sa crinière et sur sa tête, aussi …

… le lion se réveilla.

Far away and long ago, as a lion lay asleep, a little mouse ran up his tail. She ran onto his back and up his mane and onto his head …

… so that the lion woke up.

Le lion attrapa la souris et, la tenant
dans ses grandes griffes, rugit de colère :
« Comment oses-tu me réveiller !
Ne sais-tu pas que je suis le Roi des
Animaux ? Et je vais te manger ! »

The lion grabbed the mouse and, holding her in
his large claws, roared in anger: "How dare you
wake me up! Don't you know that I am the
King of the Beasts? And I shall eat you!"

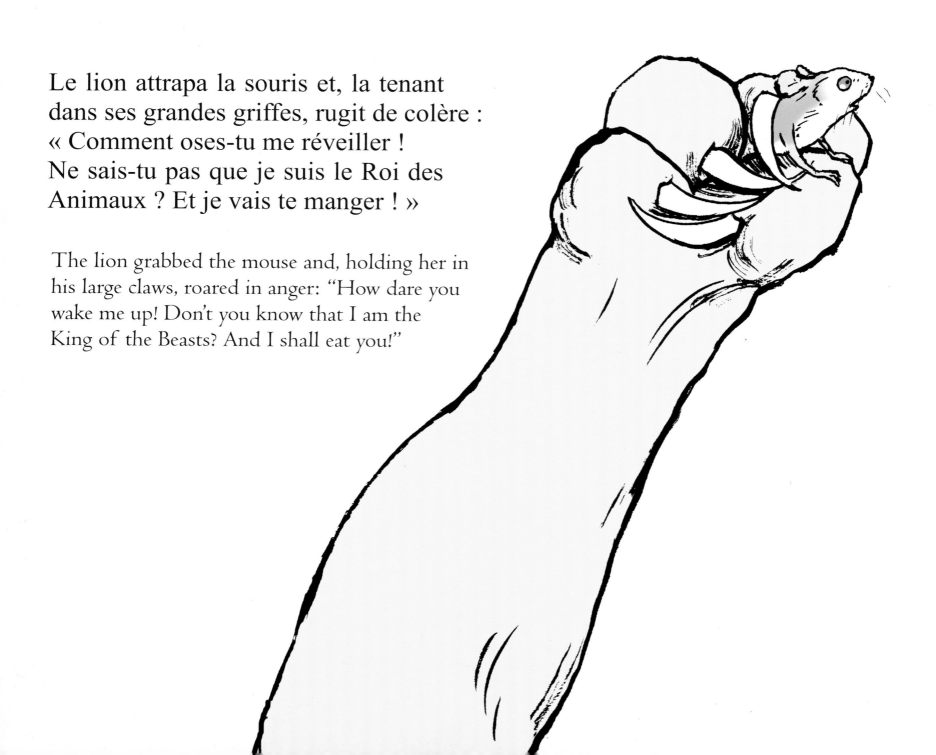

La souris implora le lion de la laisser partir. « S'il vous plaît, ne me mangez pas, Votre Majesté ! Laissez-moi partir - et je vous promets que je serai votre amie à tout jamais. Qui sait, un jour je pourrais vous sauver la vie. »

The mouse begged the lion to let her go. "Please don't eat me Your Majesty! Please let me go - and I promise I will be your friend forever. Who knows, one day I might even save your life."

Le lion regarda la minuscule souris et éclata de rire. « Toi me sauver la vie ?
Quelle idée saugrenue ! Mais tu m'as fait rire et mis de bonne humeur.
Aussi je vais te laisser partir. »
Et le lion ouvrit ses griffes et libéra la souris.

The lion looked at the tiny mouse and burst out laughing. "*You* save *my* life?
What a silly idea! But you have made me laugh and put me into a good mood.
So I shall let you go."
And the lion opened his claws and set the mouse free.

Seulement quelques jours plus tard, le lion fut pris dans un filet de chasseur. Même avec sa taille et sa force il ne pouvait pas se libérer. Il lâcha un rugissement de colère qui fit trembler la terre.

It was only a few days later that the lion was trapped by a hunter's net.
Even with all his size and strength he could not break free.
He let out a roar of rage that shook the earth.

Tous les animaux entendirent son cri …

All the animals heard his cry ...

mais uniquement la minuscule souris courut dans la direction du rugissement.
« Je vais vous aider, Votre Majesté » dit la souris. « Vous m'avez laissée
partir et ne m'avez pas mangée. Aussi maintenant je suis votre amie et aide
pour la vie. »

but only the tiny mouse ran in the direction of the lion's roar.
"I will help you, Your Majesty," said the mouse. "You let me go
and did not eat me. So now I am your friend and helper for life."

Elle commença immédiatement à ronger
les cordes qui emprisonnaient le lion.

She immediately began gnawing at the ropes that bound the lion.

La minuscule souris grignota jusqu'au coucher du soleil. Elle rongeait alors que la lune et les étoiles apparurent dans le ciel. Finalement, juste avant que le soleil ne se lève à nouveau, le Roi des Animaux fut enfin libre.

The tiny mouse nibbled until the sun went down.
She gnawed as the moon and stars appeared in the sky.
Finally, just before the sun rose again,
the King of the Beasts was free at last.

« N'avais-je pas raison, Votre Majesté ? » dit la petite souris.
« Ce fut à mon tour de vous aider. »
Le lion ne riait pas de la petite souris maintenant, mais dit,
« Je ne croyais pas que tu pourrais m'être utile, petite souris,
mais aujourd'hui tu m'as sauvé la vie. »

"Was I not right, Your Majesty?" said the little mouse.
"It was my turn to help you."
The lion did not laugh at the little mouse now,
but said, "I did not believe that you could be
of use to me, little mouse, but today
you saved my life."

Teacher's Notes

The Lion and the Mouse

Read the story. Explain that we can write our own fable by changing the characters.

Discuss the different animals you could use, for instance would a dog rescue a cat? What kind of situation could they be in that a dog might rescue a cat?

Write an example together as a class, then, give the children the opportunity to write their own fable. Children who need support could be provided with a writing frame.

As a whole class play a clapping, rhythm game on various words in the text working out how many syllables they have.

Get the children to imagine that they are the lion. They are so happy that the mouse rescued them that they want to have a party to say thank you. Who would they invite? What kind of food might they serve? Get the children to draw the different foods or if they are older to plan their own menu.

The Hare's Revenge

Many countries have versions of this story including India, Tibet and Sri Lanka. Look at a map and show the children the countries.

Look at the pictures with the children and compare the countries that the lions live in – one is an arid desert area and the other is the lush green countryside of Malaysia.

Children can write their own fables by changing the setting of this story. Think about what kinds of animals you would find in a different setting. For example, how about 'The Hedgehog's Revenge', starring a hedgehog and a fox, living near a farm.

The hare thinks the lion is a bully and that he always gets others to do things for him. Discuss with the children different ways that the lion could be stopped from bullying. The children could role play different ways of dealing with the bullying lion.

La Revanche du Lièvre
Une Fable Malaisienne

The Hare's Revenge
A Malaysian Fable

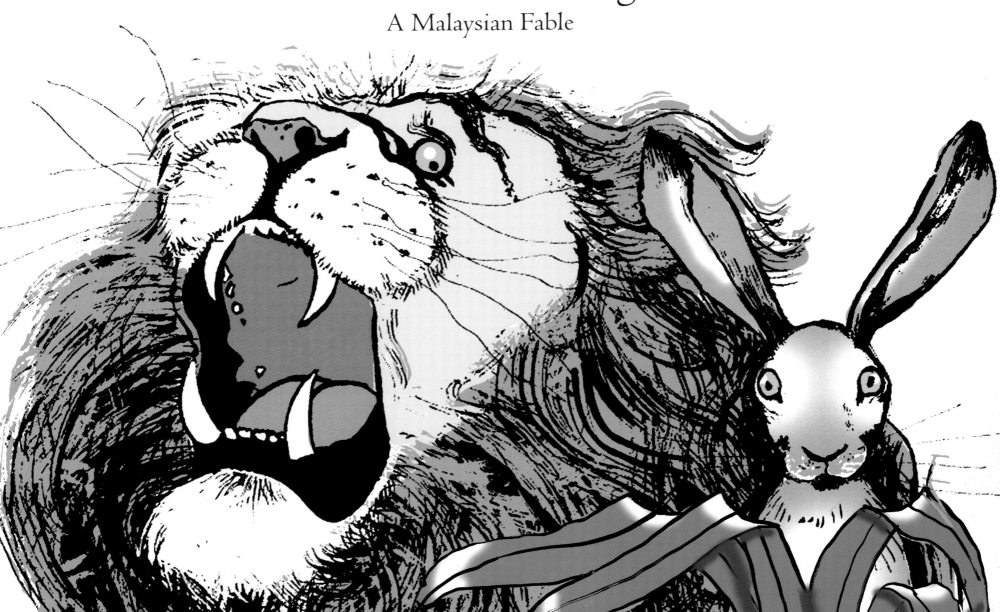

Un lièvre et un lion étaient voisins.

« Je suis le Roi des Bois, » se vantait le lion. « Je suis fort et courageux et personne ne peut me défier. »

« Oui, Votre Majesté, » répondait le lièvre d'une petite voix apeurée. Puis le lion rugissait jusqu'à ce que les oreilles du lièvre deviennent douloureuses, et il se mettait en colère jusqu'à ce que le lièvre se sente très malheureux.

A hare and a lion were neighbours.

"I am the King of the Woods," the lion would boast. "I am strong and brave and no one can challenge me."

"Yes Your Majesty," the hare would reply in a small, frightened voice. Then the lion would roar until the hare's ears hurt, and he would rage until the hare felt very unhappy.

Finalement, le lièvre pensa, « J'en ai assez ! Ce lion est un tyran et un imbécile et je dois prendre ma revanche. »
Aussi, il alla vers le lion et dit, « Bonjour Votre Majesté. J'ai rencontré un lion qui vous ressemblait. Ce lion a dit qu'IL était le roi de ces bois, et qu'il chasserait quiconque le défierait. »

Finally, the hare thought, "I can stand it no longer.
That lion is a bully and a fool and I must get my revenge."
So, he went to the lion and said, "Good day,
Your Majesty. I've met a lion who looks
exactly like you. This lion said HE
was the king of these woods and
that he would see off anyone
who challenged him."

« Oh oh, » dit le lion. « Ne m'as-tu pas mentionné ? »

« Oui, je l'ai fait, » le lièvre répondit. « Mais cela aurait été mieux si je ne l'avais pas fait. Quand j'ai décrit quelle force vous aviez il a ricané et dit des choses très grossières. Il a même dit qu'il ne *vous* prendrait pas comme son serviteur ! »

"Oho," the lion said. "Didn't you mention *me* to him?"

"Yes, I did," the hare replied. "But it would have been better if I hadn't. When I described how strong you were, he just sneered. And he said some very rude things. He even said that he wouldn't take *you* for his servant!"

Le lion s'enflamma. « Où est-il ? Où est-il ? Si je pouvais trouver ce lion, » rugit-il, « je lui apprendrais très vite qui est le Roi de ces Bois. »
« Si Votre Majesté voulait, » répondit le lièvre, « je pourrais vous emmener à sa cachette. »

The lion flew into a rage. "Where is he? Where is he? If I could find that lion," he roared, "I would soon teach him who is King of these Woods."
"If Your Majesty would like," answered the hare, "I could take you to his hiding place."

Aussi le lièvre emmena le lion à un puits profond et dit, « Il est au fond. »

So the hare took the lion to a deep well and said, "He is down there."

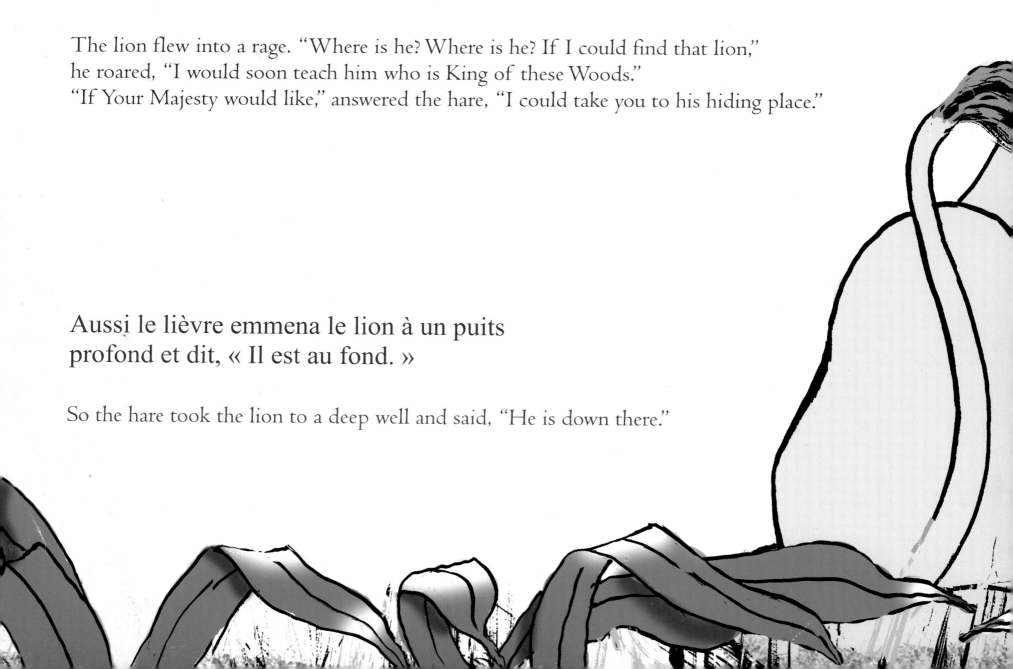

Le lion lança un regard furieux dans le puits.
Là, il y avait un énorme lion furieux, le regardant.
Le lion rugit, et un rugissement encore plus fort remonta du puits.

The lion glared angrily into the well.
There, was a huge ferocious lion, glaring back at him.
The lion roared, and an even louder roar echoed up
from within the well.

Rageur, le lion bondit dans les airs et se
jeta lui-même au lion furieux du puits.

Filled with rage the lion sprang into the air and
flung himself at the ferocious lion in the well.

De plus en plus bas il tomba et ne fut plus jamais vu.

Down and

    down and

        down he fell

            never to be seen again.

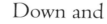

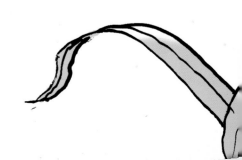

Et voici comment le lièvre eut sa revanche.

And that was how the hare had his revenge.